OOPS! ACCIDENTAL INVENTIONS

MICROWAVE OVENS

by Catherine C. Finan

Consultant: Beth Gambro
Reading Specialist, Yorkville, Illinois

BEARPORT
PUBLISHING

Minneapolis, Minnesota

Teaching Tips

Before Reading

- Look at the cover of the book. Discuss the picture and the title.
- Ask readers to brainstorm a list of what they already know about microwaves. What can they expect to see in this book?
- Go on a picture walk, looking through the pictures to discuss vocabulary and make predictions about the text.

During Reading

- Read for purpose. Encourage readers to think about how they use microwaves as they are reading.
- Ask readers to look for the details of the book. What happened to take the microwave from an accident to an everyday appliance?
- If readers encounter an unknown word, ask them to look at the sounds in the word. Then, ask them to look at the rest of the page. Are there any clues to help them understand?

After Reading

- Encourage readers to pick a buddy and reread the book together.
- Ask readers to name two things that happened when the microwave was being developed. Find the pages that tell about these things.
- Ask readers to write or draw something they learned about the creation of the microwave.

Credits:
Cover and title page, © kazoka30/iStock and © Grassetto/iStock; 3, © Grassetto/iStock; 5, © Wojciech Kozielczyk/iStock; 7, © Kong Ding Chek/iStock; 8, © Andy_Oxley/iStock; 9, © Raimond Spekking/Wikimedia Creative Commons license 3.0; 11, © Anterovium/Shutterstock; 12, © Tanya Sid/Shutterstock; 13, © Luis Molinero/Shutterstock; 14–15, © irene_rebrova/iStock; 17, © Science & Society Picture Library/Getty Images; 19, © Trinity Mirror/Mirrorpix/Alamy; 21, © elgol/iStock; 22TL, © Tang Yan Song/Shutterstock; 22MR, © manonallard/iStock; 22BL, © Shawn Levin/iStock; 23TL, © PeopleImages/iStock; 23TM, © ilkermetinkursova/iStock; 23TR, © Andrey Shevchuk/iStock; 23BL, © stocknroll/iStock; 23BM, © AJ_Watt/iStock; and 23BR, © Stígur Már Karlsson/Heimsmyndir/iStock.

Library of Congress Cataloging-in-Publication Data

Names: Finan, Catherine C., 1972- author.
Title: Microwave ovens / by Catherine C. Finan.
Description: Minneapolis, Minnesota : Bearport Publishing Company, [2023] |
Series: Bearcub books. Oops! accidental inventions |
Includes bibliographical references and index.
Identifiers: LCCN 2022031739 (print) | LCCN 2022031740 (ebook) | ISBN 9798885093446 (library binding) | ISBN 9798885094665 (paperback) | ISBN 9798885095815 (ebook)
Subjects: LCSH: Microwave ovens--History--Juvenile literature.
Classification: LCC TX657.O64 F56 2023 (print) | LCC TX657.O64 (ebook) |
DDC 641.5/8--dc23/eng/20220803
LC record available at https://lccn.loc.gov/2022031739
LC ebook record available at https://lccn.loc.gov/2022031740

Copyright © 2023 Bearport Publishing Company. All rights reserved. No part of this publication may be reproduced in whole or in part, stored in any retrieval system, or transmitted in any form or by any means, electronic, mechanical, photocopying, recording, or otherwise, without written permission from the publisher.

For more information, write to Bearport Publishing, 5357 Penn Avenue South, Minneapolis, MN 55419.

Contents

A Happy Accident............... 4

Microwave Ovens Today 22

Glossary 23

Index 24

Read More 24

Learn More Online............... 24

About the Author 24

A Happy Accident

A microwave oven heats cocoa on a cold winter day.

Yum!

How did this **invention** come to be?

> Say invention like in-VEN-chuhn

Microwave ovens were made in the 1940s.

At first, people did not plan to use them to heat food.

It happened by **accident**.

Oops!

Say accident like AK-si-duhnt

Scientists were making a special **machine**.

It could find planes flying in the sky.

The machine sent out a kind of **energy** called microwaves.

Then, something odd happened.

The energy melted a candy bar!

Scientist Percy Spencer had questions.

He wanted to know what else the machine could warm.

He put corn near it.

The corn popped!

Percy did many tests with the machine.

He used it to heat up more food.

One time, he made an egg so hot it blew up!

In 1947, **restaurants** started using microwave ovens.

Then, people started getting them for their homes.

The first ovens were very big.

They cost a lot.

Over time, microwave ovens got smaller.

They cost less, too.

By the 1970s, many homes had one!

Now, many people use a microwave every day.

It is easy to heat our meals thanks to a happy accident!

Microwave Ovens Today

Today, there are microwave ovens in nine out of ten American homes.

Some microwaves can be turned on or off with just your voice!

The first microwaves were as heavy as two lions! Today, small microwaves weigh as much as two pet cats.

Glossary

accident something that is not planned

energy power that can make something work

invention something new that people have made

machine something with moving parts that does a job

restaurants places where people can go to buy and eat meals

scientists people who study the way things work

Index

candy bar 10
egg 14
energy 10
food 6, 14
home 16, 18, 22
machine 8, 10, 12, 14
restaurants 16
Spencer, Percy 12, 14

Read More

Waxman, Laura Hamilton. *Cool Kid Inventions (Lightning Bolt Books: Kids in Charge!).* Minneapolis: Lerner Publications, 2020.

Winston, Robert. *Inventors: Incredible Stories of the World's Most Ingenious Inventions.* New York: Penguin Random House, 2020.

Learn More Online

1. Go to **www.factsurfer.com** or scan the QR code below.
2. Enter "**Microwave Ovens**" into the search box.
3. Click on the cover of this book to see a list of websites.

About the Author

Catherine C. Finan is a writer in Pennsylvania. She is a big fan of how microwave ovens make cooking easier!